A Note to Parents and Caregivers:

With a focus on math, science, and social studies, *Read-it!* Readers support both the learning of content information and the extension of more complex reading skills. They encourage the development of problem-solving skills that help children expand their thinking.

 The PURPLE LEVEL presents basic topics and objects using high frequency words and simple language patterns.

 The RED LEVEL presents familiar topics using common words and repeating sentence patterns.

 The BLUE LEVEL presents new ideas using a larger vocabulary and varied sentence structure.

 The YELLOW LEVEL presents more challenging ideas, a broad vocabulary, and wide variety in sentence structure.

 The GREEN LEVEL presents more complex ideas, an extended vocabulary range, and expanded language structures.

 The ORANGE LEVEL presents a wide range of ideas and concepts using challenging vocabulary and complex language structures.

When sharing a content focused book with your child, read to find out facts and concepts, pausing often to restate and talk about the new information. The realistic story format provides an opportunity to talk about the language used, and to learn about reading to problem-solve for information. Encourage children to measure, make maps, and consider other situations that allow them to apply what they are learning.

There is no right or wrong way to share books with children. Find time to read and share new learning with your child, and pass on the legacy of literacy.

Adria F. Klein, Ph.D.
Professor Emeritus
California State University
San Bernardino, California

Editor: Christianne Jones
Designers: Hilary Wacholz and Amy Muehlenhardt
Page Production: Michelle Biedscheid
Art Director: Nathan Gassman
The illustrations in this book were created with acrylics.

Picture Window Books
5115 Excelsior Boulevard
Suite 232
Minneapolis, MN 55416
877-845-8392
www.picturewindowbooks.com

Printed in the United States of America in North Mankato, Minnesota.

Library of Congress Cataloging-in-Publication Data
Aboff, Marcie.
The tallest snowman / by Marcie Aboff ; illustrated by Sara Gray.
p. cm. — (Read-it! readers. Math)
ISBN-13: 978-1-4048-3666-2 (library binding)
ISBN-13: 978-1-4048-3670-9 (paperback)
1. Weights and measures—Juvenile literature. 2. Stature—Measurement—Juvenile
literature. 3. Measuring instruments—Juvenile literature. 4. Snowmen—Juvenile
literature. I. Gray, Sara, ill. II. Title.
QC90.6.A26 2008
530.8—dc22   2007004070

122009
005634R

The Tallest Snowman

by Marcie Aboff
illustrated by Sara Gray

Special thanks to our advisers for their expertise:

Stuart Farm, M.Ed.
Mathematics Lecturer, University of North Dakota
Grand Forks, North Dakota

Adria F. Klein, Ph.D.
Professor Emeritus, California State University
San Bernardino, California

PICTURE WINDOW BOOKS
Minneapolis, Minnesota

Dan stared out the window. It was snowing!
It was supposed to snow all week long. What
luck! School was out for holiday break, and
Dan had all week to play.

Dan put on his
heavy coat,

his hat,

and his new
snow boots.

4

His friend Sue was waiting outside for him.
She lived next door to Dan.

"It snowed almost 6 inches," said Sue.
"I measured with my ruler."

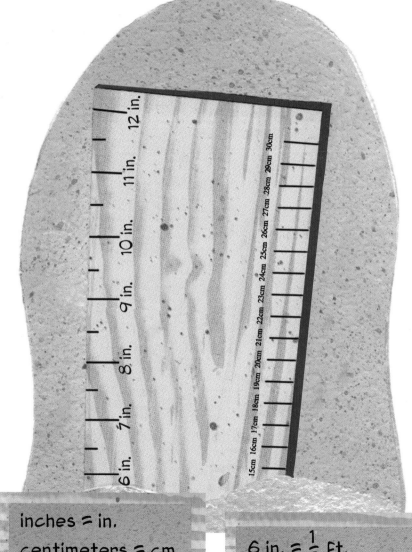

inches = in.
centimeters = cm
Foot/Feet = Ft.

6 in. = $\frac{1}{2}$ Ft.
6 in. = about 15 cm

"That's a lot of snow," said Dan. "Let's build a snowman!"

"Great idea!" said Sue.

Dan and Sue got to work. John and his friend Zack walked toward them.

"What are you little kids doing?" John asked.

Dan didn't like it when John called them "little" kids.

"We're building a really tall snowman," said Sue.

John laughed. "You guys are too little to build a really tall snowman!"

9

Dan got angry. He pointed to a tree in front of his house.

"We're building a snowman as tall as that tree!" said Dan.

"You two couldn't build a snowman as tall as any tree," John said with a laugh.

"Let's go," John said to Zack. "The little kids are playing make-believe."

"Do you really think we can build a snowman as tall as that tree?" Sue asked Dan.

"We can try," Dan said brightly.

Dan and Sue spent all morning building a snowman. They took a short break for lunch.

After lunch, they went back outside to finish the snowman. The weather turned warmer. It started to rain.

"Oh, no!" said Sue. "Our snowman is melting!"

"Don't worry," said Dan. "We'll build an even taller snowman tomorrow. It's supposed to snow all week."

The next day, Dan and Sue met outside late in the afternoon. Dan had his own ruler this time. There was about 12 inches of snow on the ground.

12 in.

30 cm

12 in. = 1 ft.
12 in. = about 30 cm

"I was worried that it wouldn't snow again," Sue said.

"I never doubted it. Let's get to work on our snowman," said Dan.

They spent the next few hours building, but their snowman still wasn't as tall as the tree.

"Let's give the snowman a tall hat," said Sue. "Maybe that will help."

"That snowman is a shrimp!" John yelled from across the street. "It's not even close to the top of the tree!"

"We're not done yet," Dan said. "We're going to make him taller tomorrow."

"Whatever," John said.

17

The snow continued the next day. The ruler wasn't long enough to measure all of the snow. Dan took out a yardstick. The yardstick was 3 feet long. The snow measured 16 inches on the yardstick.

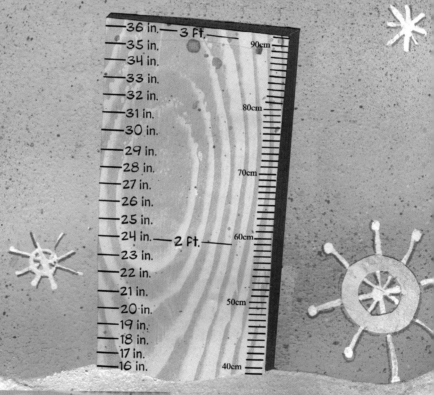

12 in. = 1 ft.
24 in. = 2 ft.
36 in. = 3 ft.

16 in. = 1 ft., 4 in.
16 in. = 40 cm

Dan and Sue took a break from building their snowman. They went sledding with their friends.

"We can finish the snowman tomorrow," said Dan. "It will still be cold tonight, so he won't melt."

It stayed cold that night, but there was a lot of wind. When Dan woke up the next morning, he went outside. The snowman's head had blown off!

"Oh, no," thought Dan. They'd have to start
the snowman all over again. Dan looked at
the tree. He wondered how tall the tree
really was.

Dan couldn't measure the tree with a ruler or a yardstick. They were too short. Together, Dan and his father measured the tree with a tape measure.

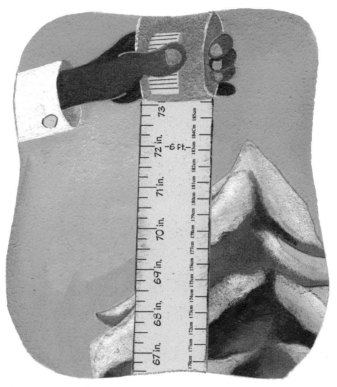

At the top of the tree, the tape measure read about 72 inches. Dan's dad said the tree was about 6 feet tall.

72 in. = 6 ft.
72 in. = about 183 cm.

"That's a really big snowman," Dan thought.
"I don't think we can do it."

It snowed for two more days. It was the wettest, heaviest, stickiest snow of the year. Dan looked outside and stared at the tree.

Suddenly, his heart raced with excitement. The tree drooped under the heavy snow.

Dan ran over to Sue's house. "We can build a snowman as tall as the tree!" he said.

"I don't think we can," said Sue sadly.

"Yes, we can, and I'll tell you why," said Dan.

He told Sue why it would be easier to build the tall snowman.

"Let's go," said Sue.

Dan and Sue ran outside. John was waiting for them.

"What happened to your snowman as tall as a tree?" he asked.

"We're going to build him right now," said Dan.

"Whatever," said John.

Dan and Sue spent all morning building the snowman. They stood on a chair to finish the top of his head.

The snowman was finally as tall as the tree!

Dan and Sue ran over to John's house.
"Look," Sue said, pointing to their
tall snowman.

"Our snowman is taller than the tree!"
said Dan.

John and Zack looked across the street.
"They're right," said Zack. "The snowman
is taller than the tree."

Zack laughed at John. "Looks like the little
kids have you beat."
"Whatever," John said.

Dan and Sue measured their snowman. He was 5 feet tall. The tree was less than 5 feet tall now that the heavy snow weighed down the branches.

60 in. = 5 Ft.
60 in. = about 152 cm.

"We said we could build a snowman as tall as a tree," said Dan.

"And we did! We can do WHATEVER we set our minds to!" said Sue.

Measurement Activity

Before they made their snowman, Dan and Sue measured each item they were going to use. Which tool do you think they used to measure each item? Why?

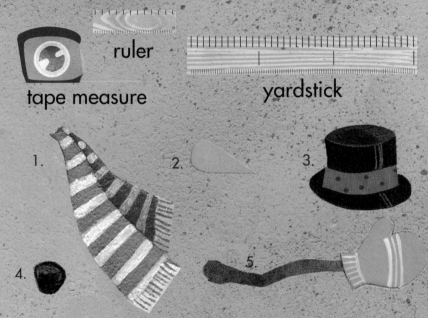

tape measure

ruler

yardstick

Answer key: 1. tape measure 2. ruler 3. yardstick 4. ruler 5. yardstick

Glossary

centimeter (cm)—unit of length in the metric system
foot (ft.)—measure of length equal to 12 inches; plural is feet
inches (in.)—measure of length that is part of a foot
ruler—a small instrument that is used to measure things; it is 12 in. (30 cm) long
tape measure—a long strip of cloth, plastic, or steel marked off in units for measuring
yardstick—a flat item one yard long and marked with units of length for measuring

To Learn More

At the Library

Aber, Linda Williams. *Carrie Measures Up!* New York: Kane
 Press, 2001.
Hightower, Susan. *Twelve Snails to One Lizard: A Tale of Mischief
 and Measurement*. New York: Simon & Schuster Books for Young
 Readers, 1997.
Pitino, Donna Marie. *Too-Tall Tina*. New York: Kane Press, 2005.

On the Web

FactHound offers a safe, fun way to find Web sites related to this book.
All of the sites on FactHound have been researched by our staff.

1. Visit *www.facthound.com*
2. Type in this special code: 1404836667
3. Click on the FETCH IT button.

Your trusty FactHound will fetch the best sites for you!

Look for all of the books in the
Read-it! Readers: Math series:

The Lemonade Standoff (math: two-digit addition without regrouping)
Mike's Mystery (math: two-digit subtraction without regrouping)
The Pizza Palace (math: fractions)
The Tallest Snowman (math: measurements)